Vigo Youth Services Juvenile Picture Boc

3922805228

W9-AAE-114

WITHDRAWN

The wonderful whisper

It began as a sigh in the faraway dark—
'I'm here!' said the Wonderful Whisper.

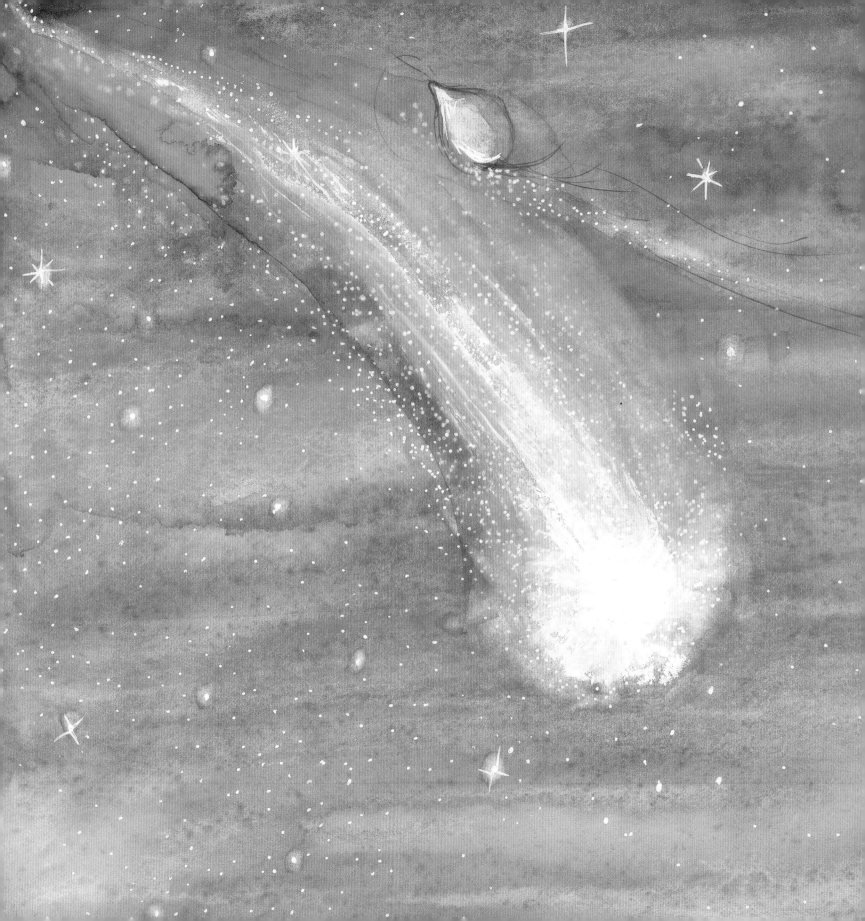

The Whisper waited with perfect calm
until it beckoned to Shooting Star,
who swept it down through the twinkling sky.

'Your spirit will shine like all the stars,'
said Star to the Wonderful Whisper.

The Whisper danced amongst the stars, and passed a thousand sparkling lights until it reached Magnificent Moon.

'Your smile will be as gentle as mine,'
said Moon to the Wonderful Whisper.

Moon made a slide of silver and light
and upon it the Whisper glided down
to the warmth of the Singing Sun.

'Your eyes will be as bright as me,'
said Sun to the Wonderful Whisper.

Sun sent the Whisper on its way,
on a river of fire and rays of heat,
to the place of the Cuddling Clouds.

'Your touch will be as soft as ours,'
said the Clouds to the Wonderful Whisper.

With fingers of fog and veils of mist
the cloud cradled the Whisper close,
all the way to the Swaying Sea.

'Your laugh is as sparkling as the waves,'
said Sea to the Wonderful Whisper.

The sea tumbled and roared and played
as it carried the Whisper on soaring waves
to the shores of Enduring Earth.

'Your heart is as loving as the land,'
said Earth to the Wonderful Whisper.

Word of the Whisper echoed far

and the animals raised their heads to hear,

then set off on claw and paw and wing
to learn of the Wonderful Whisper.

Birds flew across sunset skies,

lizards scurried through desert sands,
bears loped and wolves ran
to find the Wonderful Whisper.

They arrived in twos and threes and crowds
to see the one with the wonderful name—
they pressed and nudged and peered and craned
to see the Wonderful Whisper.

'Where is it? What is it? Who is it?' they cried.

Whose spirit
shines like the stars?

Whose smile is as
gentle as the moon?

Whose eyes glow
brightly like the sun?

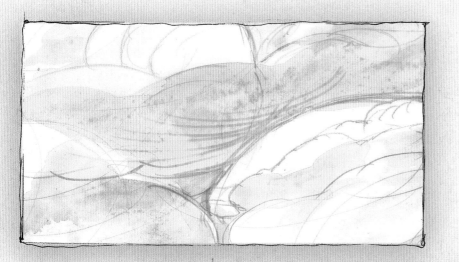

Whose touch is softer
than a cloud?

Whose laugh is as
sparkling as the waves?

And whose heart is
as strong as the earth?

Do you know who it is?

It is you!

For Bel and all the Wonderful Whispers of the world—EK

For Mum, Isabella and Rose—AP

Little Hare Books
an imprint of
Hardie Grant Egmont
Ground Floor, Building 1, 658 Church Street
Richmond, Victoria 3121, Australia

www.littleharebooks.com

Text copyright © Ezekiel Kwaymullina 2013
Illustrations copyright © Anna Pignataro 2013

First published 2013

All rights reserved. No part of this publication may be reproduced, stored
in a retrieval system or transmitted in any form or by any means, electronic,
mechanical, photocopying, recording or otherwise, without the prior
written permission of the publisher.

Cataloguing-in-Publication details are available from the
National Library of Australia

978-1-921894-16-9 (hbk.)

Designed by Vida & Luke Kelly
Produced by Pica Digital, Singapore
Printed through Asia Pacific Offset
Printed in Shen Zhen, Guangdong Province, China

5 4 3 2 1

*The illustrations in this book were created with a
combination of pencil, watercolour and gouache.*